Tears And Laughter

Stories Only A Pastor Can Tell

Neal R. Boese

Fairway Press, Lima, Ohio

TEARS AND LAUGHTER

FIRST EDITION
Copyright © 2003 by
Neal R. Boese

All rights reserved. No portion of this book may be reproduced or utilized in any form or by any means, electronic or mechanical including photocopying, without permission in writing from the publisher. Inquiries should be addressed to: Fairway Press, 517 South Main Street, Lima, Ohio 45802-4503.

Library of Congress Catalog Card Number: 2003112875

ISBN 0-7880-2102-8   PRINTED IN U.S.A.

Gifts from God come in many ways. One way is through people whose lives affect ours. In this book you will meet some special people whose contribution to my life cannot be measured. I dedicate this book to them.

　　　　　　　　　　　　Neal R. Boese

Table Of Contents

Foreword   7

CHAPTER ONE   9
   The Telephone Rang

CHAPTER TWO   17
   My Little Girl

CHAPTER THREE   25
   Quite A Night

CHAPTER FOUR   35
   A Simple Scene

CHAPTER FIVE   45
   Always A Smile

CHAPTER SIX   51
   A Check To Give

CHAPTER SEVEN   59
   Not Good Enough

CHAPTER EIGHT 　It's Dark Down There	67
CHAPTER NINE 　Just Six Years Old	75
CHAPTER TEN 　Keep Your Eyes Open	81
CHAPTER ELEVEN 　You Just Never Know	87
CHAPTER TWELVE 　Who Could Imagine?	93
Conclusion	101

Foreword

There are certain moments in life that prove to be valuable. These moments shape our thinking and add important dimensions and understandings. Some of these moments cause us to laugh. Other moments bring us to tears. But one thing about these moments: they can be incredible learning opportunities.

I have been a Lutheran pastor for 38 years. I served congregations in Texas, Nebraska, Michigan, and Kentucky. Along with being a parish pastor, I have been and continue to be a consultant to congregations and church leaders throughout the United States and Canada. During my journey I have experienced special moments that have given me new insights. They taught me to look at life, ministry, myself, and others in a different way. They taught me about the church and the role that I was to play in the church. They taught me about life and how to deal with so much that life presents. And these moments, however personal, are moments I would like to share with you. As I share these moments, I will also share what I learned. I hope what I learned will assist you in your own life journey.

I am grateful to congregations, pastors, church leaders, and friends who have contributed to this journey. I am especially indebted to my family who have supported me throughout the journey.

I have been privileged to speak at numerous gatherings involving pastors and church leaders. I have written three books on the subjects of outreach and spiritual gifts. In these gatherings and through these books I shared some of the following stories. If you have heard or read these stories before, please recognize that I cannot assume the reader of this book has done the same. Whether or not the stories are old or new, it is my hope that what I learned will be what you gain from this book. I am privileged that you will take time to share in my life's journey.

CHAPTER ONE

The Telephone Rang

It was a hot, sticky summer afternoon in Dallas, Texas. Two months before, I had graduated from Hamma Seminary in Springfield, Ohio, packed my suitcases, and moved to Texas. As I opened the door to the parsonage, the phone was ringing. I answered the phone and was surprised by what I heard. "You are needed at Southwest Hospital. My grandfather has just a few more hours to live. Could you come?" "Certainly," I said and hung up. As I put the phone down and turned toward the door, I felt faint and thought that I was going to pass out. Even though it was hot outside, I knew it wasn't the heat getting to me. It was the realization that I did not have the faintest idea what I was going to do once I reached the hospital and nothing that I had experienced before prepared me for what lay ahead.

To understand my thinking, let's go back a few years. In fact, let's go back to my childhood years. My father and mother were both Lutheran and active in First Lutheran Church, Nashville, Tennessee. My father served as President of the congregation and my mother taught a ladies Bible class for 35 years. Without a doubt, the church was the center of their lives.

Therefore the church was my second home. I served as an altar boy, never missed a Sunday School or Confirmation class, and was there with my parents in the fourth pew on the right side of the sanctuary every Sunday.

I was active in the church youth group and one year served as the President. As President, one of my responsibilities was to give the sermon on Youth Sunday. Youth Sunday was that once a year occasion when the young people of the church led the entire worship service. During that service, the pastor would generally sit in the back ready to leave if it was awful. But the fact is, everyone in the congregation liked the service as they could see their children up front, and also the service was generally short. From what I understand, the all-time shortest service was seventeen minutes.

On the Sunday I was to give the sermon, I was nervous. But as I gave the sermon, the nervousness left and I enjoyed doing it. Following the service, all who participated stood in line as people left the auditorium and shook hands with us. Some told me that my sermon was so good that I ought to be a pastor. Even though they said the same thing to anyone who had ever given the sermon, even though it didn't matter if the sermon made any sense or even if you passed out halfway through it, I took their words very seriously. Through the encouragement of my family and congregation I decided to become a pastor.

I went to a Lutheran university, graduated, and went directly to seminary. During my college days, I went to chapel every week. Even though college chapel was compulsory, it still sounds pretty good to say that I went every week. Once in seminary, each student was given the chance to serve a vacant congregation on the weekend. There you gained some experience but also made a little money.

At the end of my second year, I had the opportunity of going on internship. Internship is an opportunity to serve for one year in a congregation and get a feel for what congregational life is all about. On the surface this sounds like a good idea, but I didn't take advantage of it for two reasons. First, I was told that most students who went on internship never returned to seminary. Secondly, I had grown up in a Lutheran church, gone to a Lutheran college, married a Lutheran girl, went to a Lutheran seminary, and had the belief that my background and experience in the church were enough. After all I had been President of the youth group, went to chapel every week while in college, served in congregations during seminary, and through the years had been to an incredible number of services. No matter what would occur in a congregation, I would be able to handle it. Or so I thought!

Back to that hot, sticky day in Texas. With my wealth of experience in congregational work, I had to figure out what to do. I knew that I had to find the hospital. After a few wrong turns, I found it and went in the main door. Immediately there was a smell that made me sick, and before going to the front desk, I went into the bathroom and threw up. Then I went back to the front desk and was given the room number. Feeling sick again, I went back to the bathroom where once again I threw up, and then I went to the room.

The door to the room was closed and there was a note on the door that said, "Check with the nurses." Since I was feeling a whole lot better, I didn't think that was necessary, so I went in. There was only one bed in the room and a large number of people were standing around it. As I walked in, they all turned and looked at me, and my heart almost stopped. What do I say? And very honestly I can't remember exactly what was said, but we can be assured that it wasn't anything too significant.

I was there for a while with much of the time spent trying to figure out how to leave. Finally the opportunity arose and so I said my good-byes and started toward the door. "Pastor," someone said, "couldn't you have a prayer with us?" Again, my heart sank. I didn't have a book of prayers and had never made up a prayer in my life. So I gave my first spontaneous prayer. I can't remember exactly what I said, but this part I will never forget. I finished my prayer with the words, "and, O Lord, may Thy will be done." I opened my eyes just as everyone else opened their eyes, and at that precise moment, the one ill closed his eyes for good. Right then and there he died. They looked at him and then they looked at me. I looked at him and I looked at them, and my first thought was, "Lord, your timing is awful."

****

Within two weeks of my arrival, I knew that I had no experience that would help this congregation. I supposed I could do all right on Sunday morning, but when it came to dealing with crisis intervention and pastoral care, I was in deep trouble. So what was I to do? I guess I could have limped along, but thanks be to God I did something else. I called the President of the congregation and asked him to contact the church council and other influential members. "Ask them," I said, "to meet you and me at the church tomorrow evening."

The next evening we met together. I shared with them my anxieties, my inadequacies in dealing with congregational matters, and told them that if they wanted to get someone else I would understand. They looked at me and almost in one voice, said, "No, that isn't the answer. What can we do to help?" Their response speaks volumes as to the kind of people they were. They thanked me for my candor and set about doing what they could to help me. One member, a former social worker, agreed to go with me to the hospitals. She said that she would give the prayers if I wanted, but I decided to try to handle that myself. Another member took two days off work, came into the office, organized it, and gave me a crash course on management. And we went from there.

I stayed in this congregation for four years. During that time we grew from sixty members to over 400 members. We built a new sanctuary and developed a social ministry program that through the years has been of assistance to literally thousands of people. I would like to say that it was my outstanding leadership that made this happen, but it wasn't that at all. It was the fact that together we made it happen. Together we carried out the ministry of the congregation.

Everyone had their place and their responsibility and incredible things occurred.

It was from a sense of panic that I went to these members and asked for help. But in the process I gained their respect, and most importantly, it opened the door for corporate ministry. No one laughed at me or felt as if they had a loser on their hands. They accepted me as I was and we joined hands.

When I left seminary I believed that as Pastor I was totally responsible for everything in the congregation. As a shepherd is totally responsible for the welfare of the sheep, I was totally responsible for the welfare of the congregation. If anything went wrong, it was my fault. If anyone got mad or left the congregation, it was because of me. If the congregation had a problem, it was my problem. I was there to carry the burden for the whole congregation.

But I quickly learned that this perception is wrong. I am not the only one our Lord brings to a congregation. God brings us all together for the purpose of joining in ministry. The more we join in ministry, the closer we come to fulfilling mission. What an important lesson to learn, and I am grateful I was able to learn this so early in ministry. I am also grateful our Lord brought together in the first congregation people who took me by the hand and led me in a wonderful journey of service.

I learned how wonderful and caring people can be. Especially was it true of the family who surrounded that bed when I made my first hospital call. It didn't take them long to learn that I was inexperienced. But it didn't matter. They accepted me as I was and we became very close. One thing they did share with the congregation was that if ever I come and visit someone in the hospital and in my prayer conclude with the words, "may Thy will be done," the one sick might as well accept the fact that their days on earth are over.

CHAPTER TWO

My Little Girl

I can see her today. She is lying there in her purple dress. She was three years old and it was a Saturday afternoon. My daughter had gone to play with a friend. She had been gone for about an hour when I heard this loud noise. I ran out the door and saw two men from across the street racing toward the house where she was playing. Upon reaching the house they grabbed her and began working. They were attempting to reach down her throat. She had been shot.

Her friend, himself three years old, had found his father's gun lying on the dryer and, most likely thinking it was a water pistol, had aimed the gun at her head and pulled the trigger. The bullet entered below her ear and came out beneath her eye.

In moments an ambulance arrived and we went to the hospital. I was certain that she was going to die. Once we arrived at the hospital, the doctors took over and I sat with my wife in the waiting room expecting to hear at any moment that our little girl had died.

It wasn't long before the doctors came out and told us that she had been very fortunate. She would have to undergo surgery, but everything vital had been missed and they thought she would be all right. They told us if the bullet had gone a bit left, she would have been blind and if the bullet had gone a bit right, she would have been dead. I was shocked but relieved.

Yet deep down the feelings that were quickly coming to the surface were fright and anger. I was frightened by what had happen. I could have lost her. I was also angry as to the reason it had happened. That father had left a loaded gun on the dryer. What an incredibly stupid thing for someone to do.

The next few days were spent at the hospital. My wife would stay during the day and I would stay at night. One evening there came a knock on the door. It was an elderly lady. She was the grandmother of the young boy who shot Diane. She was very emotional and apologized profusely for what had happened. She expressed concern from the family and said they had called the hospital on many occasions to see how she was doing. But they could not bear coming in person to meet with me and to see Diane.

After a while she got up to leave. Before she left, she turned toward me and said, "I know how horrible this is, but there must be some reason why it happened." And then she added, "God must have had something in mind. As the Bible says, 'There is a time and a season for everything under heaven.'" And then she left.

****

Even though it was the most horrible experience I have ever gone through, there is so much that I learned. I keep remembering all the craziness that occurred those first 24 hours. I couldn't think with any coherence. Unless friends had been there to hear what the doctor was saying I would not have known the reality of the situation. In my mind, she was not going to live. After all, she had been shot through the head. Therefore when the doctors told us that she was all right, I didn't believe them. Our friends had to keep telling me that she would be all right, but it was a while before I believed them.

Through the years I have found this learning experience to be of tremendous value. I have been with families who have been thrust into trauma. As friends ask them what is happening, they are unable to tell it like it is. In hospitals, families have reported to others what the doctors have said and inevitably they did not have the real story. Without my experience with Diane, I would not have understood their inability to hear the facts.

In trauma, those involved cannot hear anything other than what they believe to be the truth. You don't have the capacity to hear what others are saying as your own mind is telling you the way it is. This is true for both a person who is the focus of the trauma and for loved ones who are there to support and love. Therefore, having someone present who is able to hear and to report to others what is actually happening has proven to be of great value both to the one in trauma and to family and friends. Since that time I have made it a point to go with a family to meet with the doctors so I can hear what is being said.

Along with being there to hear, having someone with you during crisis has another dimension. So often I have been told by individuals wanting to visit someone in crisis, "I don't know what to say. I am afraid that I will say the wrong thing." Frankly I learned that the words said make very little difference. Of course no one wants to say the wrong thing, but what makes the difference is that someone else is there.

When I think of that first day in the hospital with Diane, I must be honest and say I cannot remember one word that anyone said. But to this day I can tell you who was there. I can tell you who was the first one to walk in the door of the waiting room. I can tell you who went to get us a cup of coffee and sandwich. I can tell you who was there when the doctor told us that Diane was all right. And I can tell you who walked with us to our car when we left the hospital that evening. Sure, hearing what the doctor is saying and repeating it over and over again is invaluable, but the key is that someone who loves you is there. The ministry of presence is powerful.

Next, there is the power of touch. Some have a difficult time physically touching someone else. Especially in the pastoral ministry there has been so much said about being careful not to touch, etc. But when one is in trauma, we have to set aside the need to protect ourselves and reach out to protect someone else. A hug or a held hand is a sign that you are not alone. You are going to get through this situation. I have been with individuals and have held them tight in particular moments of pain. Never has that been any reason but to comfort. And from my experience with Diane, that hug or that kiss or that hand reaching out to hold meant more than I can possibly say. It was a sign from God that in the midst of chaos is love.

Next I want to share something that is not easy to say, but must be said if I am going to be honest. I learned what it was to hate. I had never felt such hate for a person as I felt for the father of that little boy. If I had come into contact with him, I am not sure what I would have done.

Hate was an awful feeling. It was so deep and so consuming that I felt physical pain. My heart was racing and my mind was clouded. I could not see the good things happening around me. I was snapping at everyone. I was angry with the doctors and the nurses and my wife and those people who came to be with us. I knew they were there to help, but I couldn't make myself be kind to them. I was mad and filled with hate.

This hate lasted for a period of time. I can't remember exactly how long, but during that time, I could not cope with anything good happening in my life. The horrible thing hate did was to block the possibility of receiving love and kindness from others. And not only was it dramatically impacting upon me, but certainly in my relationship with those around me.

But, thanks be to God, one day without notice, forgiveness began to occur. I began to see the situation differently. I began to understand that accidents do happen. Diane did live and she was all right, and that was the main thing. I still don't understand why that gun was left on the dryer and never will. But eventually I felt sorry for the father. I would never want to be in his shoes, and no matter how much I had hated him, it wasn't doing me any good. Somehow I was able to let go, and as that happened, the pain within me subsided. And life started to look better.

Forgiveness — we talk about, but it is the most incredible medicine one can take. In working with people who are dealing with parenting problems, marital problems, physical problems, emotional problems, or spiritual problems, the unwillingness to forgive is generally the root of the problem. Some never get past hate, and life becomes a journey of misery. Others have learned what I learned and, while we would never want to go through such an experience again, to know what it means to forgive is a powerful insight. I have also found that by sharing with others my experience with Diane and those feelings that occurred afterward, a door has been opened for care.

Finally in the midst of chaos and crisis is my Lord Jesus Christ. He is there sharing His love through friends, nurses, doctors, and even strangers. I can understand why that little boy's grandmother said what she did. It absolved her son of the responsibility. But what she said wasn't true. Jesus did not put the gun on the dryer. He did not take that gun, aim it at my little girl, and pull the trigger. Human beings did that. I am sure Jesus wept as we wept. But when it happened He moved in through the two men across the street, the ambulance drivers, doctors, nurses, and a host of friends. He moved in through flowers and notes. He loved us with touches and hugs and kisses. He was there from beginning to end, but not to hurt. He was there to heal.

CHAPTER THREE

Quite A Night

I had been serving a congregation in San Antonio, Texas, for five years. We had gained in membership and wanted to continue growing. But we recognized that some congregations reaching our size leveled off or lost members. We didn't want this to happen, so we began to study congregations that had grown consistently for a long period of time. We wanted to make sure that we had in place those programs necessary to continue our growth. We contacted our denominational headquarters and were given the names of ten congregations that were larger and had gone through at least 25 years of sustained growth.

As we began to study these congregations, we noticed that in every case spiritual gifts were mentioned as being the power that enabled the congregation to function. When I heard the words, "spiritual gifts," I immediately backed away, as all that meant to me was speaking in tongues. Speaking in tongues is a mystical experience familiar in some denominations, but not that familiar in the Lutheran Church. In those Lutheran churches where it had occurred, anger and unrest seemed to occur, so I didn't want our congregation involved in anything like this.

But we did notice something that sparked our interest. We noticed that the members of each congregation were significantly involved in the life of the congregation. They were involved not only in receiving of ministry but in the doing of ministry, and that intrigued us. In the Lutheran Church at the time, ministry was primarily done by the pastor and the membership assisted, but that was about the extent of their involvement.

So we started involving members in areas where normally they had no involvement. For instance, in the worship services, lay members started to read the lessons, give the children's sermon, and help with communion. That was brand new in the early 1970s and at first some long-time members were unsure as to its appropriateness, but overall the reaction and the response were very positive.

One night, during a council meeting, I asked if they would take ministry one step further. There were twelve members on the council. I asked each council member to take one of the months of the year and during that month to assist me with emergency calls. If I got such a call between 6:00 p.m. and 6:00 a.m. whoever was on call would go with me. The council was rather uneasy with this proposal, but did agree.

The first month went by and there was no emergency. During the second month, we had the opportunity to use this new system. I received a call and one of the charter members had died. For years she had not been aware of anything, had to be fed intravenously, and was almost a vegetable. Her death was a blessing. Regardless of the circumstances, there was loss and grief, and I was asked to visit with the family at the nursing home.

I called the council member and told her the situation and that I would be by shortly. She went with me to the home and ministered to the family in a very meaningful way. The family was appreciative of her presence and she gained much from the experience. In telling the council about her experience, she was moved to tears by all that had happened. The council was moved by her words and how meaningful the ministry had been. "At least," as one said, "it wasn't anything traumatic."

That is, until one Tuesday night, when I received a call that would change my ministry and certainly would change one council member's view of himself and his purpose for living. It was about 3:00 a.m. and the phone rang. The caller was a church member who was involved in a situation and did not have the faintest idea what to do. Could I help?

A neighbor had gone on a rampage. He had shot and killed his oldest son. He then proceeded to kill his wife. Finally he killed himself. Miraculously his other three children, who were there through the entire experience, were not shot. They were the reason for this call. Could I come and see what I could do with these children?

What an unbelievable situation. Once I was able to collect myself, I called John on the telephone. I didn't tell him the situation as I knew he would never get in the car. Once I got to his house and he was in the car, I told him what had happened. He didn't say a word as we rode toward the home of those three children. Finally after telling him the whole story, he just looked at me with the most innocent look and said, "Neal, there is something you ought to know. It isn't my month. I'm sorry, you are going to have to take me home." I burst out laughing, which, frankly, I needed at that moment, but he saw no humor in the situation.

All the way he gave one excuse after another as to why I ought to take him home. He would pass out at the sight of blood. He didn't particularly like children. He wasn't trained to handle such situations. On and on we rode, and he continued to give reasons why he shouldn't be there. Finally when we got to the house, I stopped the car, cut off the motor, looked at him, and asked if he was going to go in or not. While absolutely scared to death, he agreed to go in.

The scene was about as bad as one would imagine. There was blood on the floors and walls. Fortunately the bodies had been taken away. As we entered the house, the one who had called pointed to one of the corners of the room. There we saw the three children. They were sitting in a semi-circle, arms around each other, fists clenched, heads bowed, and not saying a word. What do you say to anyone in this situation? I went over and put my hand on one of the shoulders and there was no movement. I started to say something when John tapped me on the shoulder and said he would try to see what he could do. There were other people coming in and I went to assist them.

We were there about three hours. During that time I saw John doing some special things. One time I saw him lying on the floor with his head between two of the children. Another time I looked over, and one child was just leaning against him. I looked again and two of the children were yelling at him. At the end of the three hours all the children were moving around, crying loudly, and expressing anger and fear.

"Unbelievable," said a friend of mine who worked with children in trauma. It was unbelievable that John could have gotten those children back to reality as quickly as he did. They were catatonic when we arrived and if he had not acted as he did, they might not have come out of that situation. But John was able to do it and it was incredible to watch him at work.

I didn't see John for about two weeks and only talked with him briefly by phone. But the night of the council meeting, we were all together and I began telling the council what had happened. They were shocked and spellbound at the same time. As I pointed out all that John had done, there was a point when I paused and said to John, "I haven't asked you before: How did you know what to do?" John didn't know what I was talking about as he did not believe he had done anything amazing. I then went over ten to twelve particular ways he had dealt with the situation and not all of them were conventional yet had proved to be effective. But he didn't see any of these things as different. "I did what all the rest of you would have done." And everyone looked and said almost in unison, "No, none of us would have thought of any of the things that you did."

As the story unfolded that evening, there came a point when the room went silent. I can almost feel the goosebumps today. What was going on? For about a year as we had been studying other congregations, we kept hearing about "spiritual gifts"; about these powers that individuals are given to reach out and serve. From our understanding, spiritual gifts were the same as talents, abilities, interests. But that viewpoint didn't fit this situation.

John was an auto mechanic. He was good at fixing things. He could fix a door, paint a building, repair something that had been broken. That was his talent and interest, and he had turned this talent into an occupation. But in this circumstance, a new gift appeared. It was something he did not know existed. He had the spiritual gift of "mercy."

Several years later, as John began to work with this gift, he became involved in fixing, but not quite the kind of fixing he was doing before. On Wednesday afternoons, he would visit in the local hospital and spend his time with people who were terminally ill. As the result of several studies, it was becoming clear that terminally ill people were people being neglected. Family members, doctors, nurses, pastors, and friends would stay away from them because they wouldn't know what to say or do.

John's ministry became a ministry of listening and holding and caring. He was now fixing people's loneliness and fear. And the impact he made was immense.

****

So many discoveries have come from this experience that it is hard to pinpoint which ones have been the most important. Without question I have gained a new perspective on baptism. I have gained a new perspective on the congregation and the incredible power that many times lies dormant. I have also gained a much different view as to the role a pastor plays in the congregation. Now let me explain.

As we began to grapple with the presence of spiritual gifts, I became interested in their origin. Where did they come from? How did John acquire the gift that he was given? We talked about this many, many times. He told me that he was not aware of any moment when he felt "called" to serve God in a special way. He was never aware that God intended to use him for anything special. He certainly had a willingness to serve and thought he was doing so by working around the church. Therefore we concluded that this gift was given without John having any recollection. It was not something that came in any conscious way. It was given, but when?

The answer had to be baptism. When the waters of baptism were placed on John's head and the Spirit entered into his life, the gift of mercy was presented to him. At that moment he was called to service; he was tapped by God to be used. I had never thought of baptism in these terms. I thought of baptism in terms of original sin, the kingdom of God, and the special relationship being established between the one baptized and God and the church. But baptism as a call to service was not something that I had discovered.

Yet, I am now convinced that this is not only *a* dimension to baptism, it is *the* point. When one is baptized, one is "called" to be used. It doesn't matter whether the person wants to be called; it happens.

Think about Simon Peter and his Pentecost experience. Peter was preaching the gospel and no one was listening. The winds came, the Spirit entered, and now his preaching produced results. Peter did not ask for the Spirit nor at the time realize that it had happened, but the fact is God moved, the Spirit came, and results occurred.

The same thing happened to John. He was called to reach people who had a special need, and through the entrance of the Spirit at baptism he was equipped with the capacity to meet this need. It took him a while to discover this gift, but once discovered, incredible things happened.

Think about a congregation. Present in the congregation are baptized individuals all possessing special gifts. Imagine for a moment what would happen if everyone in the congregation knew their gift and had put it to use. You would have a powerhouse on your hands. And that is exactly what happens in congregations that realize the power of these gifts. It took me years to discover their existence, and, thanks be to God, I was there when John discovered his gift and, for me personally, helped answer a question I had been wrestling with for years.

I had been a pastor for fifteen years and never felt as if I belonged among the ordained. I passed all the tests necessary to be ordained and I served in a church and had a positive experience. But deep down I didn't feel "called." The reason was simple. First I never had any experience where I felt God speaking to me. Secondly, I could not do what I considered to be the work of a pastor. A pastor is called to share faith and walk with people through moments of crisis. In my case I didn't have a story to tell. I had no special experience when I felt God reaching out and tapping me for service. I was raised in a church and was encouraged, if not pushed, to enter the ministry. That wasn't much of a story.

But more significant was my belief that I couldn't do the things that I thought a pastor ought to do. I had a difficult time working with people in crisis. Certainly I would try, but I knew other pastors who could do it much more effectively, and always admired their ability to serve in this way. But deep inside I had the feeling that my inability to do this effectively was a sign that I shouldn't be in the ministry.

What could I do in the congregation? The only thing that I found easy and exciting was to organize. I loved to organize and carry out big projects. Mention a new building and the first thing that would come to mind was a plan to carry out the project. But that wasn't the same as walking with a person through "the valley of the shadow of death." That was real ministry; what I could do anybody could do.

My experience with John caused me to study spiritual gifts in more depth. And what I discovered was that I not only sold myself short, I sold God short. When I was baptized, God gave me the gift to plan. God gave me the ability to work through organizational procedures that allowed mission to occur. It was a gift given but not appreciated or understood. Once I learned this fact, it not only opened the door to a better understanding of what I had been given, it also opened the door to a new understanding of my role in the congregation.

Once I discovered that my gift of administration was from God and was for use in the congregation, one place this gift could be used was in helping others find their gift. Early in life I wanted to be a football coach. With my newfound gift I became a coach. Think about it. The coach doesn't play the game, but the coach's job is to put the people in the places where they can best serve the needs of the team. That is what I started doing. I developed a plan and a program to help each member understand what gift God had given them and how that gift could be used. As the plan began to be implemented, it was exciting to see ministry flourish.

Both for me and those in the congregation the most significant discovery was that we were a part of God's plan. God has tapped "little ole me" for service. I had been called, but never knew it. What a discovery! And from that point on, I never questioned my calling nor my place among the ordained.

Each of us has a gift and they are not the same. What we must do is to discover and then utilize the gift to the fullest. Wonderful things happen.

CHAPTER FOUR

A Simple Scene

Let's have a live nativity scene. Let's make it a simple scene with a manger, a few people, and a couple of animals. Since the church had a big piece of property on a major highway in Austin, Texas, I thought it could bring attention to the church and wouldn't require much time and effort. As it turned out, it brought more attention to the church than I could have imagined, and to say that it took time and effort is an understatement. Let me tell you about the time our church decided to have a true reenactment of that first holy night.

Early in October I went to our church council with my idea. As long as it wouldn't cost much money, they were all for it. So we selected a committee. In the Lutheran Church this is an absolute necessity no matter what you plan to do. The committee had their initial meeting and started talking about this "simple" live nativity scene. We talked and talked and four hours later came up with a much larger plan than what I had originally presented.

The first decision that the committee made was to have more than one scene. With such a big piece of property we couldn't just have a manger scene. No one would notice it. We could have three scenes that would stretch across the property. In the center would be the nativity scene itself. On the left side would be a scene involving the three wise men and on the right side would be a scene involving the shepherds. In the back of the scene and on a small hill leading up to one of our buildings, would be the angels. This simple nativity scene was becoming less than simple.

So, a special subcommittee was formed to build these three scenes. Lutherans know all about subcommittees as they are as much a part of church life as the worship service. But for those not familiar, a subcommittee is a special branch of the main committee charged with a particular piece of the committee's work. This important information becomes even more important as we proceed.

Now let's go back to this subcommittee brought together to build these scenes. As they were trying to envision the size that the scenes needed to be, they stood on Cameron Road, the road that fronted the church, but also the main road through the northeast part of Austin. When I say stood on Cameron Road, literally they stood on Cameron Road. I thought they would get killed. But they managed to dodge the cars that managed to dodge them and they made their determinations. As you can imagine, the scenes were now becoming larger.

When the main committee was told the size that the scenes needed to be, they realized that it would take a large number of people to build these scenes as we were running out of time. So three more subcommittees were formed. I suppose you could call them sub subcommittees. See, I told you that understanding subcommittees would be important. Each subcommittee would be in charge of building one of the scenes. So members and non-members were recruited and they went to work.

This nativity scene was now generating excitement in the congregation, in fact, so much excitement that everyone wanted to have a part. This created a new problem. How do you get everyone involved? So guess what? A new subcommittee was formed and this was a volunteer placement committee charged with the responsibility of making sure that everyone could participate.

Time was drawing near and there was still much to do. It was the first of December and publicity was needed. So we decided on the specific dates when the live nativity scene would be shown and the times for the presentations. Another subcommittee was formed to publicize this information.

Since the scene would be operating three hours each evening, a subcommittee was formed to recruit and train actors who would be in the scenes. It was decided to put people on this subcommittee who had an interest in drama, and members of our drama group became the logical choice to staff the committee. Bad decision! When they met, they decided that they couldn't have people just standing there; they had to be doing something, and it would even be better if they were talking. So we needed a script, and guess what was now formed? Another subcommittee to write the script. It was also recognized that if talking was involved, we needed to have some kind of sound system. So another subcommittee was formed to set up a sound system. Can you imagine this number of committees and subcommittees developed and fully staffed in one month? It was hard to keep track of everything.

The word got out that we were going to have a sound system and that the actors were going to do some talking, and so one evening when the main committee was meeting, our adult choir director asked to have a place on the agenda. She thought that it would be a great idea to have the choir sing in the background. She had already brought this up to the choir and they thought it was a good idea. Of course there was nothing the committee could do as the decision had been made. As most in the church know, the choir is not something to be messed with. So the choir director was thanked for her idea and asked to begin preparation.

At this point we had our one and only confrontation. When the choir met to begin preparation, a concern was expressed over the possibility of bad weather. At Christmas time in Austin, there was not much chance of snow, but there was a very good chance of rain. What if it rains and it is cold? What would happen to their voices? With all they had to do on Christmas Eve, they couldn't take the chance of losing their voices, and yet they couldn't imagine a nativity scene without their presence. So they petitioned the main committee to petition the subcommittee building the scenes to build a shelter to house the choir. The building subcommittee immediately rejected this idea as they barely had enough time to get the scenes done. "Let the choir build it themselves if they want one so badly," said the subcommittee chairman. That infuriated the choir as they weren't about to build the scene. Time was running out, so they reluctantly backed off, though they made it clear that the following year, if they were to sing, there had to be a shelter. After some negotiation, the decision was made to tape their music.

The night arrived when our live nativity scene would be shown. By this time more than 200 people were involved in one way or another and about fifty of these people were not members of the church. It was a beautiful night and everything worked to perfection. The street was crowded with cars, and police had to keep the traffic moving. Newspaper reporters interviewed several of those involved. Television stations were taping some of the scenes. I was asked by one television station to appear the next day on a local talk show.

On the second night the crowds were even larger, but this time everything did not work to perfection. It seemed to be going all right except for the winds that kept appearing and reappearing. Especially the winds were a problem for the angels. We had them on top of the hill overlooking the nativity scene. One angel was having a tough time as she was standing on a ladder high above all the other angels. By the way, this was her idea not ours. Her arms were outstretched and she was shouting, "Hosanna!" at the top of her lungs. As she was spreading her arms and speaking her word, the wind caught her wings and blew her off the ladder. All we could hear over the speaker was, "Ho sannnnnnnna," and a loud cry of pain accompanied by some words that were not in the script. Fortunately she was not hurt, but was so embarrassed that she went home.

The second problem involved our animals. They were farm animals and not used to large crowds. One of the animals was a small pony. Members whose livelihood was farming were concerned, as they knew small ponies could be spooked, and so they tied her down pretty well, or so they thought.

Picture the scene. The beautiful Christmas music is being sung in the background; all the actors are playing their parts to perfection; the crowds are growing, and suddenly the pony breaks free. Off she goes right down the middle of Cameron Road. The police frantically try to grab the rope that is dragging along behind her. The three men playing the parts of the wise men take off after the pony. With television cameras catching all of the action, this pony is racing down Cameron Road with three wise men chasing after her and the police not far behind. For two blocks the pony ran. Suddenly she veered off the road and went into an open door. That door led into the local Baptist church which at that moment was in the middle of their evening worship service.

What occurred was the first true cooperative effort between the Lutheran and Baptist churches in Austin, Texas. Even though startled, those inside the church responded quickly, and the pony was captured. The pony was then taken back to her owner who was informed that she should take her home. We all went back to the church. The Wise Men took their places and the police went back to their positions and the music started playing. It was an evening never to be forgotten.

****

What did I gain from this experience? First, I learned that there is no such thing as a "simple" live nativity scene. I suppose it could be done, but when you get a group of people together and they decide to take on a project, you never know where it is going to go even though, in this case, we only had three months to put it all together. But what I learned has proven to be very significant in my ministry. Especially have these lessons been valuable during the decade of the 1990s.

During this decade, speed has become the basis for living. We want things now. Corporations cannot make decisions that will take a long time to implement; results must occur within the quarter or their stock will suffer, and if their stock suffers, someone or ones lose their job. Fast food is a part of life as are short announcements on television. Planes are going faster as the need and desire to get there are so vitally important. Speed is what we want and what we demand.

Now let's convert this to life in the church. Short term rather than long term has taken over. When I would go to church as a child, pastors would preach forty to fifty minutes each Sunday. Today if I preached a sermon that long, by the time I finished I would probably be there by myself.

At one time planning for a major project would take months. During my childhood years, my mother was selected as the director of the church's annual smorgasbord dinner. As soon as she had accepted, I remember my dad telling me to forget seeing her for a year as she would be totally engrossed in this project. Well, it wasn't quite that bad, but almost. She spent virtually every day working on some detail of this project, and our family life was not restored until the dinner was completed.

But today life is different. Individuals will not readily agree to any project that is one year or more in length. Mobility is one reason, as people move so often that they become reluctant to commit themselves to anything that is long term. Also, individuals have so many activities going that one doesn't have the time to focus on just one activity for any length of time. The two-career family has become common and women who once provided most of the volunteer services for the church can no longer volunteer the same amount of time.

But short-term commitment is a different story. Most churches suffer from a lack of volunteers, but when you do something that will last only a few weeks or a few months, it is amazing to see the number of volunteers that step forward. In the church I last served we had a major building campaign. The length of the campaign was three months and over 200 members participated in one or more phases of the campaign. Leadership came forward and provided hours of service. But come the end of the campaign, the job was done and everyone went back to other activities. I am now wondering if the church doesn't have to go to short-term programming for many of its activities. When we go short term, the volunteers are there and the excitement is high.

This was the situation in Austin. The entire project took three months. Someone was there every day working on this scene. Everything else they had going on in life took a back seat for a short amount of time. There was a job to get done and in a matter of months it would get done.

I also learned what happens when a group of people take ownership in a project. For years, it was the pastor or the church leaders or some ad hoc group within the church that made decisions as to what needed to be done. Members carried out what a few of the members had decided. But today in most circles, there is the desire for ownership, to have a say in what happens. And usually this works well.

This was true in Austin. As more members became involved and their ideas were solicited and implemented, the project grew in proportion. If we had stayed with my idea, it would have been a simple scene and it would have been a simple scene because the idea came from one person. But more people brought more ideas, and, by the time it was over, the project was far beyond what I had imagined. In fact, the Austin City Council named it as the outstanding Christmas scene and gave us a special award. Frankly I think the local television stations helped us as they ran and reran footage of the wise men chasing that pony down the street.

What proved amazing was the identity it brought to the congregation not only within the city of Austin, but more importantly among the membership. The congregation had been in existence for years and the membership had never reached 200. Pastors had come and gone, rarely staying more than a year or so. The congregational program never varied and what had been done years before was still being done. That all changed.

Within two years after our live nativity scene the congregation had grown to 600 members. A new structure was implemented that utilized many of the members. Ideas were regularly solicited and when someone wanted to try a new idea, it was encouraged. How did this happen? It happened because congregational life became exciting, and it became exciting because all members had a say and new ideas were solicited and many were implemented. Amazing, to say the least.

And to think it all started when one night I brought together a group of people to discuss an idea that I had. Let's have a live nativity scene and let's keep it simple.

CHAPTER FIVE

Always A Smile

When I enter a new congregation, immediately I try to visit those who cannot attend church due to age or illness. David was the first such member I visited when I began my ministry in Austin, Texas. During our visit he told me his story. He had worked for one company over forty years. He worked hard, rarely taking a day off or taking time for vacation. That would come later, as he would say. He also lived during the Depression years. As a result, he became frugal, never spending any more money than necessary and certainly never spending any money on himself. That would come later.

He was given the opportunity to retire. With all his years of service and the retirement plans they offered, he decided to accept their offer and do some things he had always hoped to do. He actually spent some money on himself and this included buying a set of golf clubs. He had never played a real round of golf, but from time to time he would go to a practice range, use one of their clubs, and hit a few balls. But he didn't do this very often as a bucket of balls cost 25 cents and that was a little steep. But now he had some money saved and so he went to a local discount store and purchased his first and only set of golf clubs for $17.50. He was very proud of these clubs even though they were a little more expensive than he would have liked.

Next he and his wife decided to do some traveling. They had never been outside the city limits of Austin, and for their first trip they decided to go to San Antonio, which was only 85 miles away. They were going to the Alamo and see some shows. They were excited.

On the morning before they were to leave, he was jolted from sleep by a pain in his arm. He had never been sick and thought it strange that his arm would hurt so badly. He and his wife immediately went to their family doctor. The doctor ordered some tests to be taken. To make a long story short, he was diagnosed with cancer and given less than a year to live. All this had happened prior to my arrival in Austin.

With his situation being so critical, I visited him on a regular basis. What amazed me was his attitude. He never expressed any bitterness toward the cruel turn of fate. He didn't lament his inability to travel or play golf. Every time I visited he would have a smile on his face, and this wasn't just his way of greeting me. It was the way he greeted everyone, family and friend alike. He saw life from a different perspective, one I didn't understand.

From my perspective, life had treated him badly. Here was a man who had worked hard, never taking time for himself, never enjoying the luxuries of life, and then when the time came to enjoy some of these things, illness struck him down. I thought it was unfair and I regularly prayed to God that David would receive some miraculous cure. But as time went on, his pain grew worse and one day I received a call that he had been rushed to the hospital and might have only have a few hours to live.

I hurried to the hospital and when I walked into the room, I knew that the end was near. Here was David with several machines being used to keep him alive. His face and hands were swollen and he could hardly talk because of the pain. But when I walked in, he gave me a wave with one of his fingers and smiled. I was shocked by what I saw and the condition that he was in, and I said to him, "David, I don't see how you can keep smiling." He looked at me and said very clearly, "What else can I do when God is blessing me in so many ways?" He had said this many times before, but I assumed he was thinking of his wife, children, and friends. Right at that moment, I did not know what he meant.

At one point, David's wife was so upset that she needed to leave the room. So she went downstairs with one of their children and I stayed with David. His wife had not been gone but a few seconds when one of his nurses entered the room. She had taken care of him on previous visits. She told David that she was going off her shift, but wanted him to know that she would be thinking of him and would see him the next day. Then she reached out and in a very loving way squeezed his big toe. She left the room.

Despite the pain, David raised his head, got that big smile on his face, and said very clearly, "See why I am so blessed. God just walked in and told me that I will be fine." He laid his head on the pillow, turned a couple of times, closed his eyes, took a big breath, and went into the arms of the One who would eternally take care of him.

As I walked down the hall to find his wife and children, I saw the nurse who had come into the room. She knew what had happened by the look on my face. She started crying and said that she knew a nurse should never get emotionally involved with her patients, but David had been a person who had touched her life. And she had wanted to be there for him. I was able to tell her that she had not only been there, but had been, for David, one of God's special angels.

****

I was privileged to be in the company of a special follower of Jesus. David had no doubts that blessings were constantly being bestowed on him. He could look at the darkest of moments and see gifts of love. He could see the goodness of life. Rather than lament over the bad turns that life presented to him, he gave thanks for all the good turns that he had received.

It took a while to understand what special gift David had, but eventually I came to believe that he had the gift of "faith." He had that extra measure of faith that allowed him to see his Lord at work when others wondered if his Lord had abandoned him.

David opened my eyes to the workings of Jesus. I had been in a church all of my life. I had been seminary trained. I was serving my second congregation when I met David. But I had not seen Jesus at work in the same ways as I did after meeting him. It is not that I had never felt the presence of Jesus. I could feel the presence of Jesus in worship services, particularly at Easter and Christmas. I could feel Jesus' presence as I would give communion or baptize a child or marry a couple. At special moments such as these, the presence of Jesus would come through loud and clear.

But with David's help I now can see Jesus in other places. I look for Jesus when I have tears in my eyes, when I am hurting, or when others are hurting. I can see Jesus' love in the telephone calls that come at very opportune moments. I see Jesus' love in the plate of cookies that someone brings to make you feel a little better. I see Jesus' love in the hugs given or the tears spilled. I see Jesus in the notes that come at unexpected times. In so many ways, Jesus moves into our lives and loves us.

Through the years as I have come to understand more about this gift, I have been blessed to find others who had the same gift. And once I found them I used them in special ways. When someone is going through a difficult time, I ask the one with the gift of faith to make a visit to the one hurting. As they would visit, the gift of being able to see Jesus at work has done amazing things for others. It is one thing for a pastor to say that Jesus is with you during your difficult times, as this is somewhat expected. We represent Jesus and we are supposed to say these things. But when someone else says it and they have been through difficult times themselves, their credibility and authenticity cannot be questioned.

One of the most precious gifts God gave me was David. I have thought of him on many occasions and can't get out of my mind the words that he stated over and over again. "Just look around — Jesus is everywhere."

CHAPTER SIX

A Check To Give

Joan had been married for fifteen years and had two children. It had been a difficult marriage as her husband was one who never contributed anything for the betterment of the family. He couldn't keep a job, drank quite a bit, and was mentally abusive to both Joan and the children. I met him on several occasions and, while I normally find some redeeming value in everyone, I could find no redeeming value in this individual. He was a mean and egocentric individual. He made life miserable for anyone who came into contact with him. Even his parents would have nothing to do with him.

One day Joan called and informed me that her husband had disappeared. She had not seen him for two days and couldn't figure out where he was. She had called the police and left a missing person report, but they had uncovered nothing. It was as if he had vanished. I thought it was an act of God, and while I didn't say anything, I hoped that he would never be seen again. That turned out to be the case.

Yet in the process of leaving, he certainly left his mark. As credit card bills came in, it became apparent that just before he left he had maxed out every credit card they had. He left with money and she was left with huge bills. Despite legal efforts, she had to pay those bills. With some help from individuals in our congregation, a payment plan was established that allowed those bills to be paid over several years. It was grossly unfair that she had to pay anything, but in those days if credit cards were in both names and one could not be found, the other was liable.

So she set out to make a life for herself and her children. She worked hard and was a good mother. Without the interference of her husband, there was a joy that came into the home that was noticed clearly. But those bills provided quite a burden, and despite how much she worked, she could not make progress in paying them off. Our congregation wanted to raise some money to help her, but she wouldn't allow it. She was determined to make her own way.

So she decided to get a second job, one that could be done within the home. During the day she worked at her regular job, came home to care for her children, and when they went to bed, worked a second job. How she managed to do it was a mystery, but she was a determined person and somehow was able to keep going.

One morning, a friend of Joan's called and said that something wonderful had happened to Joan. That morning the company Joan worked for called all the employees together and announced that in a recent contest Joan had won and would be receiving $10,000. The caller was a member of our congregation. But she wanted me to pretend I didn't know anything so Joan could enjoy the excitement of surprising me.

Just a few minutes later Joan called and said that on her way home she wanted to stop by and see me. I couldn't wait to see her, and at the appointed time she was in my office. She was so excited she could barely get out the words of what had happened. And I was excited, too. Finally after all these years of one problem after another, something wonderful had happened. She told her story and at each juncture of the story I would express surprise and excitement. Finally the whole story was told and she sat there and beamed.

Then, after a few more comments, she reached into her purse and handed me an envelope. Inside the envelope was a check for $5,000 made out to the church. I didn't know what to say. We had some kind of campaign going, but she needed that money much more than we did. With the full $10,000 that had been won, she would become debt free. Finally the past, at least as far as bills were concerned, would be behind her. But she wanted to give this check, and even though I was perplexed by what she had done, she left the office with a smile that I will never forget.

****

I would like to say that it wasn't long before the lessons from this experience became clear, but to be perfectly honest, it took me a while to grasp what happened. For some time, I felt guilty about taking the money. I was shocked by her gift. I couldn't respond when she gave it. I just looked at the check and looked at her. And before I could say much of anything, she left. I wanted to chase after her and give back the money, but I just sat there.

Why didn't I go after her? Surely I could have done something. I could have tried to talk her out of giving that much money. Perhaps she could have given $1,000 rather than $5,000. That would be a tithe. That would be biblical and perhaps would have satisfied the need to give. Perhaps I should have talked about God's gifts and how this might be a gift from God to set her free. But the fact is, I didn't do anything, and, in retrospect, I am glad that I didn't.

A few years ago I went to see the motion picture *City Slickers*. It starred Billy Crystal who plays the part of Mitch, an advertizing executive who comes to believe that life is passing him by. Despite all sort of efforts, he can't shake this idea. Jack Palance plays the part of Curly, the last of the real cowboys. They are brought together because Mitch is talked into going to a dude ranch to "get back his smile."

When he and his two friends arrive at the dude ranch, they are informed that they will be going on a trail ride and Curly will be their trail boss. One day when Mitch and Curly are riding together and Mitch is griping about life in general, Curly asks him his age. Mitch tells him and Curly laughs. "You city slickers are all alike. You get all stressed out and come out here to get yourself straightened out. What you need is to understand the secret to life." "And what is that?" asks Mitch. Curly holds up one finger. "That's the answer." Mitch wonders what that one finger means. Curly proceeds to tell him that for every person there is one thing that is the most important. When you determine what that is, you will know the secret to life.

Joan had discovered the secret to life. She discovered that by putting herself second and others first she could handle anything life presents. Most people spend their lives putting themselves first. When you watch television ads, the focus is always on the self. Buy this car, and you will be somebody. Wear this fragrance, and you will be noticed. Follow this diet, and you will look good. Wear these clothes, and you will have the opposite sex falling all over you. We live in the "me" generation, and I doubt if it has been any different in the past.

And it is natural that we think this way. No one is born believing their life should be directed toward others. A baby is concerned only about the self. If a baby wants food, it doesn't matter what time of night or how inconvenient it will be for food to be obtained. The baby wants it and the baby wants it now. The baby grows into a toddler and the toddler grows into a child and the child grows into a teenager and from teenage years we become adults. And a lesson is deeply imbedded within us. Take care of yourself and do whatever it takes to get what you want.

And we build a world that evolves around us. What is interesting is that the more successful we are in building a world around us, the more miserable we become. We become miserable because everyone has to jump when we say jump and not everyone will do it. We become miserable because the more we have, the more we want. We buy a big house and there is always a bigger house. We make money and there is always someone with more money. We acquire power and there is always someone with more power. Life built around the self never is satisfactory because there is always something we don't have. There are numerous examples of people who seemingly have everything and yet are enclosed in a body that is constantly stressed and a mind that is filled with anxieties.

Think about Joan's life. She never had much of anything. She had married someone who took advantage of her. She was saddled with debts not of her doing. She had incredible responsibilities. How could she cope? She coped because she focused outside of herself. She focused on loving her children. She focused on reaching out to others. She focused on making others happy. Then one day when she won that monetary award, her first thought was not of herself, but what benefit she could provide for someone else. It never entered her mind to keep all the money for herself. She knew the secret of life. Her first thought was to give. She saw the great opportunities it would provide for others, and so with great enthusiasm and excitement, she was thrilled to give it.

Joan had been given by God the insight that everything she had was on loan. And when you think about it, that makes a great deal of sense. We enter this world with nothing materially. We leave this world and we do not take any material goods with us. What we have during that interim comes from some place, and in Joan's eyes, it comes from God.

Having that viewpoint, the next step is to use everything you have in a way that would please God. Everyone on earth is a child of God, but not everyone has the same privileges or the same material goods. Therefore, it is the responsibility of those who are blessed to be a blessing to others. It is not generosity; it is what you are called to do. Joan never thought of her gift as something generous. She saw it as an opportunity God had given. It proved to be a lesson that at least one pastor needed to learn.

CHAPTER SEVEN

Not Good Enough

I was determined to make that team. For more than a year, I practiced basketball every day. Across the street from my house was a basketball court, and there I would practice. Darkness would set in, and I would still be practicing. Dinner would be on the table, and I would be practicing. The bus would come for school, and I would be practicing. I can remember many occasions when the bus driver would yell for me to get on the bus. People would kid me about a basketball being a permanent attachment to my body. I loved to play, but more than that, I wanted to be on the school team.

I wanted to be on this team so badly that I even dreamed about playing. I dreamed about playing in front of a crowd. I would envision the score being tied and I would make the winning shot. I could see the ball leaving my hand and going through the net. I dreamed about the routine that the team followed on the day of the game. The players would be introduced at the school pep rally. They would go and have the pre-game meal. Then they would go to the locker room where they would suit up for the game.

One day, on the bulletin board, there was the announcement that I was waiting for. Tryouts for the team would begin the following week. I couldn't wait because I knew that I was ready.

On Monday afternoon, right after school about 100 of us gathered in the gym. It was assumed that players who had been on the team before would be selected, but I knew that several had graduated and the opportunity was there. Also the team had not done well the previous year, so we thought that the coach would be open to new players.

With so many trying out for the team, the coach devised a process to determine who he wanted. Games were played with three on each team. The coaches were watching carefully. Over a three-day period, I must have played twenty games. It was grueling, but at the end of the three-day period, names were called who were still in the selection process, and my name was called. Thirty players were left.

Coaches began teaching some offensive and defensive plays. Following these chalkboard sessions, we would practice against one another. I felt good as I was having no trouble with the plays being taught and I was the top scorer in most of the games. We reached a critical point when the coach cut the squad to fifteen players, five more than the number that would make the team. I was one of those selected. We played some more games and I was the leading scorer. It seemed that every time I shot the ball, it went in. One game I scored 22 of our team's 30 points. My friends started talking to me about the possibility not only of making the team, but of being a starter. I was getting so excited that when I came home from practice, I would immediately go across the street and practice some more.

We had one last game before the final cut was made and it was against another high school team. Even though I didn't start, I got into the game and scored ten points. Ten points was the most scored by any player and that included players who were in the game much longer than me.

After the game, the coach told us that the next morning a list of those who made the team would be on the school bulletin board. So I went home, very confident, but also nervous.

Morning came and upon arriving at school I immediately went to the bulletin board as I assumed the list would be posted. But it wasn't posted and no one seemed to know why the list was not there.

As I was walking out of a class, I received a message that the coach wanted to see me. I went into his office and he told me that while I had played well during the tryouts, he did not feel that I was good enough to play on his team. He had been impressed by my play and knew that a good city league would be starting soon, and if I wanted, he would tell one of the coaches about me. I stood there absolutely in shock and nodded "Yes" to his suggestion. He shook my hand and I left his office.

I was stunned, angry, and embarrassed. I was stunned because no one had played any better. I was angry especially when I found out who had made the team. Two of the players who made the team were good football players, but definitely did not play basketball that well. In fact, I had played one-on-one against both of them and they had not scored against me.

Finally, I was embarrassed since my friends were sure that I would be selected.

But they were good friends and became even more angry than I was. They wanted to start a petition to force the coach to put me on the team, but I wouldn't allow them to do it. First, it wouldn't work, and secondly, I didn't want to be a member of a team because the coach was forced to put me there. So the embarrassment subsided and, in fact, I became more popular at school as people felt that I had been shafted.

My anger also grew less because of two reasons. First, I played on the city league team and the team did well. Then the high school team itself won only three games. I can't say I was disappointed. To this day I don't know why I didn't make that team.

Years have gone by and I still remember each detail connected with this story. And I remember each detail because of one comment the coach made, "Neal," he said, "you are not good enough."

****

I learned that I wasn't good enough. And it wasn't because I would not play on that basketball team. I developed a fear that I wasn't good enough at anything. In other words, my self-worth hit bottom and stayed there for many years. Why would a situation such as that impact as it did?

It impacted because I had worked hard to make the team. I thought, "If I work this hard and can't do it, then what can I do?" This sounds silly now, but for a seventeen-year-old it was a jolt, and it affected me in many ways. Anger developed and I set out to prove that I was "good enough."

First, I set out to prove the coach was wrong. I joined the city league team and led the league in scoring. I caused people to question the coach's motivation. Eventually the coach told my father that he had made a big mistake in not putting me on that team.

But a problem developed that has affected me through the years. My worthwhileness as a person became synonymous with whether or not I won. Sports became a means to prove worth. I became not only competitive, but fanatical in my efforts to win. When I didn't win, it caused physical pain. Whenever I played any game of any kind, my worthwhileness was involved. And it carried over into my calling as a pastor.

As you remember from another story in this book, when I left seminary I went to Texas. I was one of fourteen pastors who had come to Texas either to start new missions or redevelop those that had fallen on hard times. All fourteen of us were alike. We were young, eager, and highly competitive. And the regional director of missions saw this and built on it. He developed a system that played on our competitiveness. Each month he would send a report that would list the number of calls we made, the number of new members we received, and our average worship attendance on Sunday. The way the report was presented, it was not hard to determine who was number one. It wasn't hard to determine who was making the most calls, getting the higher attendance, receiving the most new members. In other words, it told us who was the best; who was worth something; who was good enough. At least, that is the way I viewed it.

I worked hard to be number one on that chart. Most of the time I did well, but come a month when I wasn't the leader, I would be upset and determined to regain the top spot. Very frankly, we were all this way. If you were not one of the fourteen, you would have thought that we were crazy. And probably in some ways we were. But the missions were built. Most of them thrived, including the one I was in, and yet that wasn't good enough. No matter how well I did, there was always a new challenge because deep inside was the gnawing feeling that I wasn't good enough.

I could give many other examples, but the end result was always the same. When your worthwhileness is built on what you do, there is always someone who can do it better. As I look back on those times, what is interesting is that I became known throughout the church. I became known because of the work that I had done in congregations. I became known because I was elected to positions that involved a lot of responsibility. And I became known because of articles that I wrote for our national magazine. But none of this did anything for that deep-seated inner belief. My inner belief said that I was not good enough, and that inner belief ruled my life. Isn't that sad?

So what changed that inner belief? Frankly, not much, as I still have those thoughts today. But there is something else that has entered my belief system; that has forced me to rethink what I have believed about myself. Even though each chapter of this book is a new experience, I have to share another experience to make clear what I have learned.

Throughout the years as a pastor, I have networked my way to a new position. If I wanted to be pastor of another congregation, I would tell the Bishop what congregation I wanted to go to and ask for his help. I know that we are supposed to be called by Jesus to our new positions. But I never felt called, unless the call works through my own networking process, which I never considered. When I went to a new church, I had set the process into motion.

One day as I walked into my office, the phone rang. It was the assistant to the Bishop of the Michigan Synod. I had never been to Michigan in my life and had only met this assistant on one occasion. He asked me if I would be interested in coming to the Michigan Synod as the Director of Outreach. After a couple of meetings in Michigan, I decided to accept the call. There I became involved with the finest group of pastors and congregations anyone could find. This experience was mindboggling because I had nothing to do with bringing it about. It just happened.

Why did it happen? Why would something so wonderful happen to me? For someone who is not worth a whole lot, how could this happen? I was dismayed and kept waiting for the ax to drop; I kept expecting something bad to happen. But it didn't; in fact, life became better.

As this experience occurred, a new thought developed. Maybe, just maybe, I was worth something. Maybe my worth is not connected to *who* I am but *whose* I am. If something this wonderful could happen to me and I didn't do anything to cause it to happen, maybe the one bringing it about is Jesus. And if Jesus is doing all of this for me, maybe it is because He loves me. And if He loves me, I must be worth something. It is so simple to write these words, but the struggle I went through to reach this point took years.

I would love to say that no longer am I competitive, no longer is winning that important. As my golfing buddies will tell you, that isn't true. But now when I play, my worth is not at stake. I still don't like to lose, but my perspective has changed.

In the last congregation I served, I was there for thirteen years. Never have I served that long in one place, but I was not out to prove anything to anyone. I wasn't in a hurry to get something big done so I could go on to some other place to do something big in order to move on to some other place to do something even bigger. I allowed myself to smile and to take more time to enjoy all that life has to present. I now have balance in my life. I have time for myself. And above all, I know that I have a Lord who loves me.

You know what? That coach was wrong. I should have made that team. But, who cares? I am good enough. I am God's child. In the long run, that's what counts.

CHAPTER EIGHT

It's Dark Down There

One day I received a call from the local funeral director. A woman who recently moved into the area had died, and the family asked him to contact a Lutheran pastor. I went to the funeral home to meet the family.

In the course of the conversation, I learned some facts about this woman. She was 92 years old at the time of her death and had led a very active life. She spent most of her life in the northern part of the United States and had come to San Antonio to be near her children. Her church had been an integral part of her life. After meeting with the family, I decided to call the pastor of her former church.

The pastor was sorry to hear of her death as she had been very special to the congregation. She had been a Sunday school teacher and Bible study leader. Whenever the church was open for worship, she was there. The pastor added one additional fact and that had to do with her wit. She always found humor even in the worst of circumstances and she loved to play jokes on other people. They were never harmful jokes, but she loved life and she loved having a good time with others. Remember this point as we progress with the story.

We decided to have a graveside service. Following the service the family would go back to her hometown for a memorial service. The graveside service would begin at 3:00 and the cemetery was near our church. At about 2:30 I left the office and reached the cemetery in less than fifteen minutes.

When I arrived at the cemetery, I was surprised that no one was at the front gate. Normally someone would be there to take me to the grave location. I checked in the main office and the doors were locked. I was beginning to be concerned. Did I have the wrong time? I started driving through the cemetery hoping that I could find someone.

Finally I spotted one of the yard workers. He told me that no graveside service was scheduled. "But I know they said 3:00 and I know they said this cemetery." When I mentioned the name of the cemetery, he smiled and said, "You must mean the main cemetery; this is just a branch." I had no idea there was any other cemetery by the same name. The main cemetery was located on the other side of San Antonio. He called the other cemetery and, sure enough, that's where the service was to occur. By this time, it was already 3:00, and people were wondering where I was. The funeral director informed them what had happened, and that I was on the way. It would take about 45 minutes.

So off I went, and if I had traveled the speed limit, it would have taken 45 minutes, but I made it in less than thirty minutes. Even though I was embarrassed about going to the wrong cemetery, they didn't seem particularly upset. Everyone got in place and the casket was removed from the hearse. With relatives serving as pallbearers, I led the procession toward the burial plot.

The plot was located on top of a hill and there was a slight angle to where she would be laid. As I reached the top of the hill, I saw the outline of the hole covered by a green cloth and I tried to stay as close to the hole as possible so the pallbearers could get the casket in place. Just as I made my turn, the ground gave way, and I fell into the grave. It happened so fast that I didn't have any way of catching myself, and I landed on my rear end. I found out quickly that the hole was deep and it was dark down there.

I looked up and saw two faces. One was the funeral director who asked me why I was down there. I didn't think that was a particularly helpful statement under the circumstances and told him in a very direct way to get me out of there. Standing up was difficult as my feet were underneath the apparatus that was used to hold the casket.

Finally I got to my feet and I hurt all over. When I looked up, there were eight faces staring at me. The pallbearers had joined the funeral director and his assistant. A couple of guys reached down to try to get me out. There is no graceful way to be pulled out of a grave. I was dragged out. My clothes were filthy, but there was nothing I could do. The funeral director was trying to get the dirt off my back and his assistant was trying to get dirt off the front.

The family had been delayed a few moments to allow us time to put the casket in place, but now they were arriving. And what did they see? They saw a minister covered with dirt, his glasses on sideways, the casket lying on the ground away from the site, and a funeral director jumping into a grave. The funeral director was jumping into the grave because my service book and notes were still there.

As the family approached and saw what was happening, one family member started laughing. It wasn't just a snicker or a smile. He burst out laughing and the whole family started laughing. Then the pallbearers started laughing. I could not see anything humorous about the situation. Once the funeral director got my book and notes and was out of the gravesite, the pallbearers went over to get the casket. They were having a hard time picking it up because they were laughing so hard. Finally they got it in place, gave me this sheepish look, and stepped back. Most of them had to turn away, but from the shaking of their shoulders I knew what they were doing.

The family gathered around the casket. I opened the book and began the service. I had not completed the opening paragraphs when two helicopters appeared overhead. Apparently they were trying to land at nearby Randolph Air Force Base but had been put on a holding pattern. So they were flying above us and I couldn't do a thing but stop and wait. For about ten minutes we waited. Surely they could see us, I thought, but the way this day was going I shouldn't have been surprised. Finally they left and I finished the service.

I said good-bye to the family, and as I was getting into the car, one of the sons came up to me and said, "I am sure that my mother enjoyed this entire afternoon."

****

Don't ever assume that the footing around a gravesite is solid. Following that experience, no one could get me close to a gravesite when I would conduct a funeral. The casket was in place and the pallbearers had stepped back before I would get close.

Actually it took a while to learn much from this experience. I was embarrassed and didn't tell a soul what had happened. But even in a city as large as San Antonio, it didn't take long for others to find out, especially my peers. I think the funeral director had something to do with this. It seemed that anywhere I went, someone would say something about my falling into that grave. A couple of my peers suggested that I play the part of Jesus at the reenactment of the resurrection since I now had firsthand experience of what it was like to rise from the grave.

But when all is said and done, I learned something important. I learned the power and value of humor. In any profession that involves contact with people, humor is essential. Otherwise you would probably go insane. Up to this experience, humor was not a significant part of my makeup. I was intense about anything and everything. I also believed that in doing the work of the church, humor was inappropriate. When it came to the work of the church and especially during the services, I rarely grinned and definitely never laughed out loud.

I grew up during a time when anything you were doing inside a church building was considered serious. After all, it was the Lord's house and therefore you must be serious. During worship services, I never was allowed to smile or even move. You could never run inside the building nor could you talk very loudly. Therefore I grew up with the belief that the church and seriousness were synonymous.

And this view hadn't changed. It is not that I never had any fun or laughed or joked; it was simply not done in the church. When all of this happened at the cemetery and I recognized the humor that was coming from it, I was forced to do one of two things: get mad when they kidded me, or laugh with them and have fun with it. The latter is what I eventually was able to do and that proved to be a wise decision.

I will never forget the first time I used this story in a sermon. The congregation was not used to humor. Every sermon had been serious and whenever someone would smile at something I had said, my look told them that their smile was inappropriate. This had been the case for years, but one Sunday it changed, and it was a change for the better.

On this Sunday, I decided to give my sermon from a different location. Instead of standing behind the pulpit with my notes in front of me, I stood in the middle of the altar area and started talking. I had no notes. I must tell you that I was terrified. I thought that I would forget something. But I decided that if I was going to tell this story, it would lose something if I read from a manuscript and stood behind a pulpit.

As I got into the story, one member of the congregation started smiling, and since I was smiling, others thought it was appropriate to do so as well. As I told more of the story, the smiles changed into open laughter. At the end of the sermon when I told them what one of my colleagues had said about my playing Jesus at the resurrection, they let loose with laughter that you could have heard blocks away. When I said, "Amen," the congregation stood and applauded. I couldn't believe what happened.

On that day my approach to sermons changed in three ways. First, I came out from behind the pulpit and used very few notes. I cannot tell you how many positive comments I received. Instead of preaching at them, they felt as if I was identifying with them, getting into their heads and lives. Secondly, I started using personal situations and experiences. I shared my life and my own conflicts with faith. I shared with them stories that caused them to laugh and cry. Finally, I started using humor. I didn't use it all the time, but often enough to make a point.

The use of humor has opened doors. It lets people know that you are human and even though you wear a robe and stand behind an altar, you are no different than they are. It also lets people know that it is okay to laugh. In fact, it would do people a lot of spiritual good if they would laugh. Life is taken too seriously, and I have concluded that the less we laugh, the less we enjoy life. The more we laugh, the more we appreciate all that God has in mind for us.

On that day when I went to her funeral service, I am sure that the woman being buried was watching this whole thing. In fact, I am sure she orchestrated the whole thing. Actually,

I don't believe this, but let's put it this way: if she could have, she would have. And as horrible as life was that day, in the long run it was funny.

CHAPTER NINE

Just Six Years Old

When she left home to visit a friend, everything in the household was normal. When she returned, the household was far from normal. As she walked in the door, her grandmother picked her up and held her tightly. Her mother was surrounded by friends and family and they were crying. When her mother saw her, she came over and, choking down tears, told her the reason that so many people were there. Her father had been killed in a tractor accident.

For two days the congregation and I reached out to this family in many ways. The family was dealing with shock and grief, and they were also having to make some decisions. Many of them had to do with the funeral. Since all family members lived within a short distance of the home, there was no need to delay the funeral, and it was set for two days following the accident.

As the mother was dealing with her grief, she was also wrestling with a decision she had to make with regard to her daughter. Should she take her to the funeral or should she keep her at home? In this community, the visitation and funeral were both held at the church the day of the funeral. The visitation began two hours before the funeral. About an hour before the visitation, it was customary for the family to come to pay their final respects. This would be the one and only time they would see the deceased before the burial.

So what was the mother to do? To help her make a decision, she talked with the ones closest to her. She went to her mother and asked what she thought. The mother thought it would be best if the little girl was kept at home. By doing this she would remember her father as he was, full of life and health.

Then she went to her sister, and the sister thought just the opposite. Take her to the funeral. Let her see her father as he is. By doing this, the sister counseled, she would not spend life wondering what he looked like. She would be a part of everything and that would be important.

When the day of the funeral came, I was not sure what she was going to do. On the day before when I had talked with her, she had made one decision, and then later on that day, she had changed her mind. Everyone she asked had very strong opinions, and the more opinions she was given, the more confused she became. I did not know what she was going to do.

The custom in that community was for the funeral director to bring the casket to the church about an hour before the family would arrive. They would place the casket and the flowers in a specially designated area not far from the worship area. On the morning of the funeral, I was with the funeral director making sure that everything was in its proper place.

As we were talking, we became aware that someone was standing behind us. When we turned, we saw the mother holding her little girl. No one else was with her. She had decided to come to the church early and with her daughter see her husband before anyone else arrived.

The funeral director and I stepped back to give some room. We wanted to be close, but we also wanted them to have some privacy. The mother, holding her daughter, went to the casket and stood there. The little girl didn't say a word. There were no tears, nor was there any movement in her body. The mother later told me that she thought her daughter was in shock because of her lack of movement. Finally, after what seemed like an eternity, the daughter raised up and out of her pocket pulled a stick of chewing gum. She took the gum and placed it in her father's pocket. She straightened up and said, "Goodbye, Daddy. I'll see you tomorrow."

****

There were many people, when told this story, who believed that this little girl did not understand what had happened. She was reacting and did it in a very sweet way. But I am not so sure. The longer it has been since this happened, the more I believe she knew more than most of us. In her own way, she knew that her daddy would be all right. She was confident that her father was in good care. She was sure that she would see him some day. With her childlike faith, she had a confidence that most of us would like to have. And the smile she gave her mother is a smile I will never forget.

In the kind of cynical world you and I live, it's refreshing when we are exposed to something that denotes positive thinking. The naysayers point out the negative. No matter what anyone does, according to them, it is done for a selfish reason. When anyone expresses faith, they are put down as ones who are whistling in the dark. When someone sees something positive happening in the world, immediately the negative is expressed.

I was visiting someone in the hospital. He was going to undergo surgery the next day and, of course, was expressing his anxiety. We talked about his faith and we talked about the procedure that would be used, and we talked about the excellence of the medical staff. While we were talking, the doctor came in and expressed those same thoughts. When the doctor left, the patient was beginning to develop confidence that he would make it through and back to a normal life (which he did, by the way).

As I was about to leave, a friend of his came in the room. We started talking and he asked how things looked for the surgery. The patient told him what the doctor said and how positive everyone seemed to be. Immediately upon hearing this, the visitor said, "Oh, you can't always believe a doctor. After all, they bury their mistakes." What feeling of confidence the patient had was immediately lost as his friend had "told him the facts."

Why is it that "the facts" are always negative? They are negative because they are the only facts people believe. Look around and see how the negative impacts. A person is arrested and immediately it is assumed that guilty will be the verdict. Gossip abounds and, regardless of who spreads it, the gossip is assumed to be true.

For a couple of years I served on the Board of Directors for a local social service agency. A few years ago we had some problems. We were forced to close the agency for a couple of months while some changes were made. The local papers ran stories about what had happened. They didn't bother to talk with the board members; rather they wrote what they thought would be newsworthy and, of course, that was the negative. The articles all denounced everything we had done and the majority of articles did not have any semblance to the truth. But it didn't matter. If it was in the paper, it was true. And it seemed the more negative the article, the more it would be believed. The Board went through some very difficult times that would not have occurred if the truth and the positive reason for our actions had been told.

Sorry to say, I also get caught up in the negative. For years I have been visited by people with emergency needs. They tell me their story and it is filled with heartache and crisis. I believed their stories. I have no idea how many personal and church dollars I used trying to meet the need. I felt for their need and wanted to help. Then I found that in one case after another I was being taken and the need really wasn't there. I had one experience when I was talking with one of the family members and outside my office another family member was stealing something from the church. I finally reached the point where I didn't believe anyone. I was always looking for the catch. I expected a con artist. But knowing that some might be telling the truth, I eventually had everyone meet with my assistant who might be able to look at the situation with more objectivity. I was just so focused on the negative.

With all that has happened in my life and with all the negative situations that I have had to deal with, this little girl presented a picture I needed to see. She has forced me to look at life differently. Rather than focus on the negative, I try to focus on the positive. Instead of assuming the worst, I look for the best. Rather than look for the lie, I try to find the truth.

This incident also made me recognize an important element of faith. Faith is believing in that which you can't see. All we see is what happens here on earth. We read about heaven. We think about the next life. But this is the only life we know for sure. That little girl believed in heaven and she believed in a loving God who would take care of her father. She also believed that on one of these tomorrows, she would see her father. Oh, for a childlike faith.

CHAPTER TEN

Keep Your Eyes Open

Even though it took place many years ago and many miles from where I now live, I am still affected by what happened. Her name was Alice and when I arrived in Austin to begin my ministry, she was one I got to know right away. She was in the midst of a difficult situation. Shortly before I arrived, her husband had become ill at work and passed out. He was immediately taken to the hospital and placed in the intensive care unit because his breathing was labored. The doctors were perplexed by his condition as they couldn't find anything in their initial testing that would cause this kind of reaction. Finally, after several weeks of testing and retesting, they discovered a brain tumor.

The only course of action was surgery. While the doctors expressed concern with surgery, they all agreed that it was the only chance he had. Early one morning, we all gathered at the hospital to be with him before surgery and to sit together during the long ordeal — and it was an ordeal. The surgery lasted all day and it was touch and go. From time to time the nurse in charge would tell us how things were going, and she wasn't always that optimistic. Finally the word came that the surgery had been completed. When the doctors finished and he was taken to ICU, they would be out to talk with us. When the doctors came out, we could tell that they didn't have great news. While they were pleased that they had gotten the tumor, they were very concerned that they had to cut into the area of the brain that affected his motor skills. They did not know what the long-term effects would be.

It didn't take long to recognize the long-term effects. First, he was unable to use his legs and would be in a wheelchair. Secondly, his arm strength was such that he could barely grip anything. Finally and most devastating, his inner spirit was destroyed. His worthwhileness had been based on what he could produce, and now he was unable to produce anything. He was a nothing, a nobody, and absolutely of no use to anyone. Despite what Alice would say, what I would say, what his friends would say, it made no difference; bitterness and anger would dominate the rest of his life.

And so Alice set aside her career and her interests and turned into a full-time caretaker. And her life was a "living hell." No matter what she did, it was wrong. Now matter how much she told him that he was loved, he didn't believe it. No matter how hard she worked at getting him to do something for himself, it didn't work. Finally one day he made a decision, and the decision was to quit on life. And from that day on, he did not utter one word, nor would he attempt to assist anyone trying to take care of him. He was breathing but he wasn't living. He had decided to die and if his body wanted to keep going that was fine; as far as his mind was concerned, life was over.

Many of us tried to help. We would go and be with him so she could go to the store or get out of the house for a while. But it was hard to stay long as either he didn't say a thing or, early on, he would say things that were not what anyone wanted to hear. And while it was rough on us, we couldn't imagine what it was for Alice. How could she go through something like that and keep her sanity? Above all, how could she go through this and keep her faith?

As friends would gather, inevitably Alice and her husband would come into the conversation. We would pray for some change to come over him, some happiness to come into both their lives. We prayed for strength for Alice as we knew she didn't have much left. Constantly the question was raised, "How can she keep going? She needs something miraculous to happen." And one day it happened.

I would generally see her during the afternoon. One day when I stopped in, she was so at ease, so at peace. I thought her husband had come around, was responding to the love she was providing, but that wasn't it. As I sat down, she said some things that really jolted me. "Pastor, this morning I was feeling down." As if she didn't have plenty of reason. "Then the doorbell rang and Jesus came in to see me." When she said this I have to admit my first thought was that she had broken.

She could see the startled look in my eye. "Let me tell you what happened. Early this morning, the doorbell rang. When I opened the door, it was my neighbor. We have not been close through the years nor had she come by in the past few months. But she told me that early that morning, something told her to make a plate of cookies and bring it over and give me a hug. Pastor, that was Jesus who told her and that was Jesus who came through the door. And when she left, I went into the kitchen and my eyes fell on the pile of cards that had come to me over the past few months. As I read them, it was Jesus telling me that He was with me and He was with my husband and that it would be all right."

From that day on, all noticed a change in Alice. She still had difficulties taking care of her husband, but there was a peace, a calmness that took over. I would like to say that it affected her husband and he changed, but that didn't happen. A year or so after this happening, he died and he died without ever saying another word. But he died with Alice beside him, holding his limp hand, and saying the Lord's Prayer. Finally he was at peace, but beside him was someone who was also at peace. And it began one day when the doorbell rang.

****

Alice taught us many things, but above all she taught us unconditional love. We talk about it. We think we are open to giving it, but in reality most of us love but expect to be loved in return. We tell someone that we love them, but we expect to hear the same in return. We do something nice for someone and expect that person to do something nice or nicer for us. We give expecting to receive and likewise we love expecting to be loved.

What Alice taught us was that loving unconditionally creates an incredible sense of peace because you are giving without expecting anything in return. No one can take away the good feeling because your giving is the only thing that is involved. You expect nothing. Therefore no one can disappoint you.

I am sure that Alice's husband could have cared less if she had left him. He could have cared less if she would have gotten angry with him for not responding to her love. He could have gone on with his life with or without her. But that didn't matter to Alice. She loved him and that was all there was to it.

That is what was so unique about Jesus. People could mock Him, attempt to trick Him, disappoint Him, even crucify Him, but nothing could take His love for them away. It is because He expected nothing in return. He simply loved and the return He received was a sense of peace.

Alice was at peace and in the process of gaining that peace, she witnessed for us what it means to give unconditional love.

CHAPTER ELEVEN

You Just Never Know

Most pastors will tell you that a wedding can be a nightmare. Certainly a man and woman vowing before God that they will share life with each other is holy and humbling, so if all a pastor had to do was the wedding, it would not be so bad. But that isn't true. Even though the service is the most important aspect of the entire event, for all too many couples it is the prelude for what will occur later.

I have conducted over 900 weddings in my ministry and each is special and has its own uniqueness, but there is one that stands out. It stands out for several reasons. First, the bride-to-be was not a member of the church. Secondly, she scheduled the wedding four years in advance. She told me that her grandparents had been married on a particular day in June; her parents had been married on that same day thirty years later, and four years from then, it would be thirty years after her parents married, and she wanted that particular date. I asked how the groom-to-be felt about waiting four years, and her response was, "Oh, I haven't met him yet, but I will by that time." Normally I don't do weddings for those who are not members of the congregation, but in this case, I wanted to see what would happen. So I agreed, even though I must admit I didn't have a calendar for four years later nor did I expect it to happen.

One day in April four years later the phone rang and it was this young lady who quickly reminded me of our meeting and my promise to marry them. The day would be the third Saturday in June, and we set a time for them to come and meet with me.

At exactly the appointed hour my secretary ushered them into my office with a look on her face that told me something unusual was about to happen.

The nicely-dressed bride-to-be walked in first. She immediately came over to shake my hand. Behind her came an elderly man who I assumed was her grandfather. With cane in hand, he came over to shake my hand, and it was then I discovered that he wasn't her grandfather. He was the groom.

I tried to remain cool, but I did not achieve my goal. They saw the shocked look on my face and sat down to explain why they desired to be married. She had graduated from college with a degree in gerontology. (I know you are thinking, I must be making this whole thing up. But, frankly, the truth is better than anything I could make up.) After graduation she had gone to work in an assisted living complex. In this complex she worked with people on one particular floor. Here she met this man. She would talk with him for hours and he always had time and interest. "He cared about me in a way that was special."

At this point, I was getting a headache. Here was a young lady determined to get married on a particular date; she had met someone who talked with her, and in her mind he had become the chosen one.

I asked him to tell me a little bit about himself. He had never been married and assumed it would never happen since he was 72 years old. But if this was what she wanted, then it was fine with him. They couldn't move into his apartment at the complex, but there was a house nearby owned by the retirement village and management said they could live there.

My premarital counseling sessions generally cover several areas. We talk about family, religious beliefs, sex, and finances. But in this case I didn't quite know how to approach any of these subjects. She didn't want children, so that took care of that subject. I had no desire to get into the sexual aspect of their relationship, so that took care of another subject. They had both been Lutheran and were part of the worshiping community at the assisted living complex, so that covered the third area, and finally, he had plenty of money and no one to spend it on, so he was happy that she would make good use of it.

With those subjects covered, I asked if there was any subject we ought to discuss, and they named one. They were having a problem with her parents. The parents were not coming to the wedding. Her father could not imagine his daughter marrying someone 21 years older than he was. I was having trouble with that myself. The parents called me several times in hopes that I would talk the couple out of the marriage. They were perturbed that I would consider officiating at the service. But as I told them, I don't make judgments as to whether or not a couple should get married. That is up to them. My role is to assist them in getting married and to establish a relationship.

The day of the wedding came. All the guests were ushered to their seats by the oldest ushering crew I have ever witnessed. Among the guests, there were the young and the old. There were children and people in wheelchairs. The bridal party came in a limousine and the groomsmen came in the assisted living bus.

Her father came to the wedding and walked her down the aisle, but I do not believe that his tears were tears of joy. By the time the wedding was over, there was not a dry eye in the crowd. Those from the rest home were crying out loud and those on the bride's side didn't know whether to laugh or cry. It was incredible. I couldn't think of an adequate Bible story to tell as I didn't know of any couple where one was 72 and the other was 30. When each said, "I do," that completed the most unusual wedding I had ever conducted.

****

You just never know. You think you have seen it all, then one day you find something new. With this couple, everything within me said to say, "No," to officiating at the wedding. I had this feeling that the marriage would not last and that they were together for the wrong reasons. I never heard "love" mentioned, only compatibility. I never heard them talk about the future, only the present. I was lost trying to figure out the logic of this union.

But look what happened! First of all, he lived to be 93, and they were happy years. Secondly, they had a child one year after they were married. After the wedding I had moved to another congregation in another state and discovered this fact when I was called to do the funeral of the groom.

I met his son and he told me about his father. First, he never thought of his father as being older, but did have to spend time explaining that it was not his grandfather or great-grandfather who was with him; it was his father. Secondly, even though his father was much older, he was the only parent among his friends who always was there. His father took him to school and brought him home. He attended every event at school and became involved in school activities. In fact, during his high school years when his father was 87 years old, he was named the "parent of the year" for his participation in school activities. As the young man told me, "Once you got past the gray hair and the cane, everyone found that I had the greatest dad one could have."

His mother worked full-time once their son was in school and eventually became the director of that assisted living center. Not only was she talented and committed, she knew in a very personal way what life for an older person was like. But as she quickly cautioned me, she never thought of him as an older person; he was Jack. She also told me that through the years their love blossomed into a union that she hoped was pleasing to God, as it certainly was a gift to them.

I want to add that Jack became very close to his wife's parents. In fact when he died, her father, who had almost refused to attend the wedding, spoke at the funeral and was a pallbearer.

I would like to say that I knew this would happen, but it turned out much differently than I had expected. It also turned out to be a prime example of what marriage is about.

Out of this experience I learned that my practice of not determining whether a couple should or should not get married was correct. Nothing in my experience told me that this marriage would work, but it did. Nothing in my experience told me that this marriage would last, but it did. Nothing in my experience told me that they were together for the right reasons, but they were. In other words, what I saw on the outside was not what was on the inside, and what was on the inside was the most important.

Therefore, one morning when your secretary comes in with this stricken look on her face, don't immediately assume it will be all bad, for you just never know.

CHAPTER TWELVE

Who Could Imagine?

It was a beautiful Wednesday in September. My buddies and I were finishing a round of golf when my cell phone rang. It was my wife Marsha. "When you finish the round, could you come home?" This was unusual as normally I would finish playing golf, have something to eat, and then go teach a class. But it was obvious that she needed me, and so I immediately left the course.

When I walked in the door, she was sitting in a chair crying. "What is wrong? Are you ill?" "No," she said, "I just got back from the doctor and I'm pregnant." It wasn't long before I was sitting in a chair with tears running down my face. "You must be kidding. How could this happen?" And she just looked at me.

For many people this would be a wonderfully exciting moment, but for us that was not the case. I was 52 years old and had two grown daughters. My wife was younger than I, had a son, but never wanted or expected to have another child. We just sat there in shock.

All sorts of things ran through my head. I couldn't go through this again. I loved raising my daughters, but that was years ago. I didn't want that kind of responsibility. I wanted to travel and relax and enjoy the rest of my life. In this day and age with all that kids have to deal with, I would not know what to do. And then what struck me was the realization that when I would be seventy, he or she would be graduating from high school. Would I be alive?

As you can imagine, it didn't take long for the word to spread. Friends didn't know what to say. Some came up, shook my hand, and walked away shaking their heads. Others tried to tell us how exciting this would be, but they were not persuasive. Still others made comments that they thought were funny, but really were cruel. Our children reacted in different ways. My older daughter cried, my younger daughter smiled, and my stepson thought it was great as now he could have someone to boss around.

As depressed as I was when Marsha told me about the pregnancy, I was even more depressed when I thought of the role a husband plays in delivery. It was a role different than the time when my two girls were born. When they were born, I was with my wife in the labor room, but when it came time for delivery I went to the waiting room. And that was fine because what happened in the labor room was all I could handle.

Today husbands are in the labor and delivery room. I knew this from all the births in the congregation. But I was glad that when my children were born, it was different. Maybe, I thought, she would want to do it the old way. Maybe she would know that I had never done such a thing. Maybe I will be in the waiting room. Maybe!

That thought ended when one evening she told me about classes that the hospital gave for expectant mothers and fathers. They would go through step by step what would happen. We could pre-register and husbands would be taught how to help their wives. And then, she said, we will be prepared when we go together into delivery. So much for the "maybe's."

The day for the class came and we walked in the classroom door. We immediately noticed that the room was filled with twenty-year-olds. They greeted us warmly, thinking we were the teachers. When the real teacher came in, they thought I must be my wife's father. When they found out I was the husband, no one said a word, but just looked at each other.

I suppose these classes are good, but I was not adjusting to them very well. They wanted the fathers to practice the breathing techniques their wives would be using in labor. Every time we would start the exercise, I would burst out laughing because I felt so ridiculous. No matter what we tried, I would get it wrong and Marsha was not happy with me. We made it through but I'm thankful there was no final exam.

It was early one morning. Marsha had gone into labor and we were waiting to go to the hospital. I was going through my class notes wishing I had paid more attention. Then the time came and we were off to the hospital. It was only a mile or so away, so it didn't take any time to get there. We had pre-registered and gone through the procedures of what we were to do, and everything went smoothly. She was in the labor room less than twenty minutes after we left home.

The labor was going well. At least for me it was. I was trying to breathe with her, and all she could do was to breathe, cry, and laugh. She kept saying, "Stop breathing," and I wasn't sure what she meant. But I was breathing with her and also filling out this chart. In the class, we were told to keep track of the contractions, and I had a chart to end all charts. I even had visions that one day it would be the chart every husband would use. I could sell the copyright and make a fortune. The nurses told me it was the most detailed chart they had ever seen and would be very helpful to the doctor. When the doctor came in, I proudly gave him the chart. He looked at it for a second, wadded it up and threw it into the wastebasket. So much for my copyright idea.

We noticed that the nurses were coming in more than we thought was necessary. They kept looking at the monitors and then rushing out. Neither of us thought too much about it, but the more it happened the more concerned we became.

Then the doctor put his head in the door to see how things were going. He looked at the monitor and suddenly got this panicked look on his face and shouted at the top of his lungs, "Good God, we are losing the mother and baby! Get her to surgery." He looked at me, pointed a finger and said, "You stay right here." The doctor proceeded to turn the bed around as fast as possible and out the door he went. Marsha looked back at me with this frightened look, a look I will never forget.

So there I was sitting alone in the room with "code blue" echoing up and down the halls. I was scared to death. I walked out of the room and down to the nurses' station. I found no one. There wasn't a person in the halls, and even though it was 4 a.m., I still expected to see somebody. It was like everyone left and I was there alone.

I went back to the room wondering if I had lost Marsha and the baby. The only thoughts that came to mind were thoughts of fear and anguish. It seemed like hours, but in reality about thirty minutes passed when I heard footsteps. I stood up and in walked a nurse I knew from my days visiting in the hospital. She had a big smile on her face, hugged me tightly, and said, "Neal, everything is fine. Marsha is doing well and you are the father of a handsome son. What are you going to name him?" I could barely breathe. I had trouble even saying the words. "Mitchell Lawrence," I said, "but we will call him Mitch."

****

Last week Mitch celebrated his twelfth birthday and I can't imagine life without Mitch. I think of all the despair that we felt those nine months before his birth. I think of those first three months after his birth where we rarely slept through a night. But today we know that Mitch was and is a special gift that God presented at an unexpected time of life.

We had raised our children and were quite proud of them. We looked forward to those years when we wouldn't have all the responsibilities we had before. We could retire or work part-time, and relax, something that had not happened very often through the years. The days ahead would be ours to do as we please. But God obviously had something else in mind.

Today our time is spent differently from what we had anticipated. Our days are built around this bundle of joy and enthusiasm. We run around like a taxi cab, taking him to his ball practice, his game, his school event, his activity, and on and on we go. I am the official score keeper for his baseball team and Marsha was a home room mother and volunteers at the school. Nights are spent doing homework, playing ball, and watching a movie. For a number of years, every Monday I would leave the church about 4 p.m., go home, and pick up Mitch. Together we would go to the airport. We would park in long-term parking, take the bus to the terminal, take the train to the concourse, buy a pizza, and watch the planes take off and land. What a joy and what a blessing were those days.

Not long ago a friend of mine told me something very interesting. "Twelve years ago when you told me that you and Marsha were having a baby, I felt so bad for you. I felt bad because I thought your coming years would be difficult and you wouldn't be able to enjoy them. Were we wrong. You are the blessed ones."

What did I learn from this experience? I learned that no matter how hard you try, you cannot map out your road ahead. Sure, we make plans, but changes occur. And they are changes that may seem impossible at the time, but may also lead into a world that opens up incredible doors.

I also learned how much love God has for us. So often we fail to see this love because what is happening seems so overwhelming. But God presents us what we can handle. Never did I think we could handle this change in life plans, but the fact is, this was not a change. The road that we were to lead went exactly the direction it was supposed to go. We thought we knew the direction, but we were only kidding ourselves. The best we can do is to know there is a way, and every so often get a clue as to the direction it is taking. But don't get too comfortable. For undoubtedly it will change.

"What will you name him?" asked the nurse.

"Mitchell Lawrence will be his name, but we will call him Mitch."

Conclusion

Twelve stories do not make up a person's life, but, in my case, these stories have shaped the direction. I concluded with the story about Mitch because his story graphically displays the point of this book:

Who could have imagined:
- Being lost in a new job could lead to the resurrection of a congregation
- Your little girl being shot could bring about a new understanding of love and forgiveness
- A horrible tragedy would open eyes as to the incredible power that is within
- A less than simple nativity scene could change the direction and future of a congregation
- Lying on a death bed would cause others to see the continuing presence of God
- Within the arena of hostility and anger comes the answer to inner peace
- Getting cut from a team leads to a sense of worth
- Falling into a gravesite changes one's style of preaching
- Grieving hearts are opened to Jesus' love by the faith of a little child
- Unconditional love shows itself in the most unlikely of places

- A marriage making no sense becomes a model for marriage
- A couple in despair finds undeniable joy

Life is difficult because it is so unpredictable. You never know what is going to happen. But, on the other hand, not knowing what will happen brings excitement and wonderful opportunities.

Above all, what I learned is this: In the most unexpected times and places, open your eyes and look around, for it's here that Jesus displays his incredible love.

About The Author

Neal R. Boese has been a Lutheran pastor for 38 years. He served congregations in Texas, Nebraska, and Kentucky. He has also served as the Director of Evangelism in the Michigan Synod, LCA and as the Evangelism Consultant for the Indiana-Kentucky Synod, ELCA. Presently he is the Evangelism Consultant for the Southern Ohio Synod, ELCA

Other books by Neal Boese include *Why Can't We Grow? We Can!* published in 1989, *Seven Steps and You Will Grow* published in 1991, and *Spiritual Gifts, Power That Drives the Congregation* published in 1995.

Along with serving in congregations and as an evangelism consultant, he does outreach and spiritual gift seminars throughout the United States. He can be contacted by e-mail at nboese1210@aol.com or by writing him at Seven Steps Ministries, Box 18036, Erlanger, Kentucky 41018.

He resides in Edgewood, Kentucky, with his wife Marsha, son Mitchell, and stepson Brian. He has two daughters, Diane Boese-Koch and Karen Bunnell, two sons-in-law, Troy and Eric, and three grandchildren, David, Molly, and Luke.

Order Form

Copies of this book may be ordered by writing:

SEVEN STEPS MINISTRIES
BOX 18036
ERLANGER, KENTUCKY 41018

OR

FAIRWAY PRESS
P. O. BOX 4503
517 S. MAIN STREET
LIMA, OHIO 45802-4503

BOOK COST IS $9.95
PLUS POSTAGE AND HANDLING

Postage and Handling Charges
$9 to $29   add $2.50
$30 to $50   add $3.50

I wish to order _____ copy/copies of the book *Tears and Laughter*. Enclosed is my check for _____ that includes postage and handling. Please allow 2-3 weeks for delivery.